NOW EVERYBODY REALLY HATES ME

by Jane Read Martin and Patricia Marx

illustrated by Roz Chast

HarperCollinsPublishers

Library of Congress Cataloging-in-Publication Data
Martin, Jane Read.
  Now everybody really hates me / by Jane Read Martin and Patricia
Marx ; illustrated by Roz Chast.
      p.   cm.
  Summary: Confined to her room for punishment, a child muses about
staying there forever.
  ISBN 0-06-021293-4. — ISBN 0-06-021294-2 (lib. bdg.)
  [1. Punishment—Fiction.]   I. Marx, Patricia (Patricia A.)   II. Chast,
Roz, ill.   III. Title.
PZ7.M363166No   1993   92-13075
[E]—dc20   CIP
                                                              AC

Typography by Christine Kettner
1   2   3   4   5   6   7   8   9   10
❖
First Edition

To Our Parents
—JRM and PM

For Ian and Nina
—RC

I am in my room and I am never coming out.

Here is what my parents say: The reason I am in
my room is because I hit my brother Theodore on the
head and called him a dumbbell in front of everyone
at his birthday party.

Here is what I say:

#1) I did not hit Theodore. I touched him hard.

#2) I did not call him a dumbbell. I called him a dumb head.

#3) Which I didn't mean even though it is true.

#4) All I wanted to do was to look at his new dump truck for one measly second.

Just a few minutes ago I made my mind up. I will stay in my room for the rest of my life.

Unless we are having something good to eat tonight.
If it's good it will be my last meal.

But if it's something bad, I will never come out again.

In my room I am going to stay up really really really really late. It will be so late when I go to bed that it will be the next day.

I will never sleep in my bed again. I will sleep on the floor at all times. Except when I sleep in the fort in my closet. And I will put thumbtacks around my fort to make it Theodore-proof.

I will never speak English again. I will speak in a code that only I will understand.

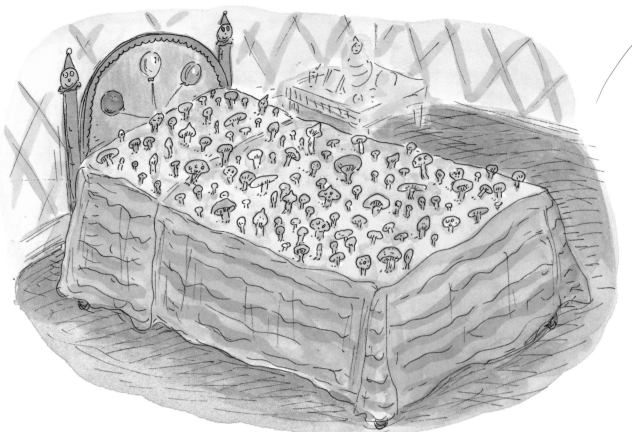

I will never clean up, and in a few days poisonous mushrooms will grow on my bed. Meanwhile, Theodore will have to do all my chores, including

and

EMPTY THE WASTEBASKET

SET THE TABLE

But I will still get my allowance.

I will walk Sarge. Because Sarge is the only one who
loves me even though he does not talk. How will I
walk Sarge without leaving my room? Easy.

I will never come out of my room. Unless I am allowed to wear my red loafers all the time, even though they are bad for my feet.

If I am not allowed to wear my red loafers all the time, I will cry forever. Which will be so noisy that everybody will hold their ears all day long.

If I ever do leave my room, I will live with somebody else's parents. Maybe Sondra's. They let you have as much gum as you want.

What about Lisa's sleep-over next Saturday? I will go—but I will not tell anybody I am leaving my room. How?

I will dig a tunnel. What will I dig it with?

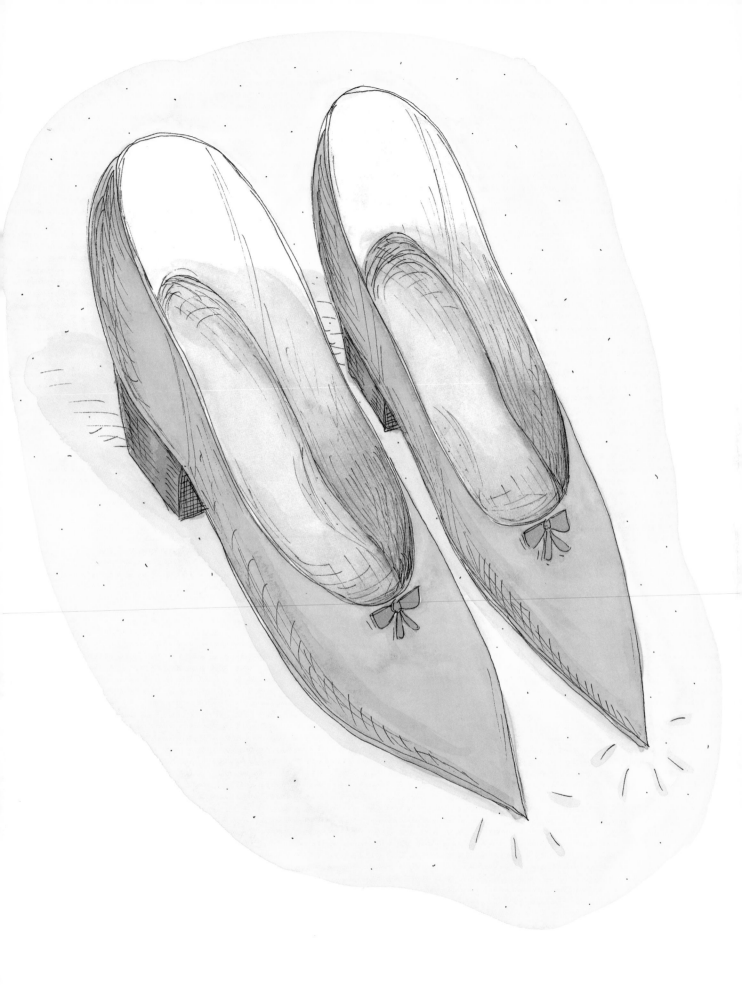

My pointy dress-up shoes.

Tonight at exactly 9:02, I will start my mission. I will begin to dig my Tunnel to Freedom. The Tunnel will go through my wall next to the yellow table and under Theodore's bathroom. That is where I will pull the plug in his bathtub drain so that he is freezing cold. And naked (ha ha!).

Then the Tunnel will proceed directly under Theodore's room so that I can steal all his stupid birthday presents except for the clothes, which I hope he gets a lot of.

Next I will stop under the kitchen, where I will pick up two poached yolks on toast, canned spaghetti, soda, and cupcakes. I will eat this for breakfast even though I will not eat breakfast until lunchtime, when Theodore will have to eat liver and brussels sprouts and skim milk with no dessert whatsoever.

Finally, the Tunnel will go to my parents' room, where I will leave them a good-bye note. The note will say:

By my calculations, it will take precisely 837 years, 4 months, 3 weeks, 6 days, 7 hours, 5 minutes, and 23 seconds to get out of my house. But it will be worth it.

Speaking of calculations, I have now been in my room for exactly 53 minutes and 29 seconds.

I think I will sing "Happy Birthday" to Theodore:
   "NOT Happy Birthday to you,
   NOT Happy Birthday to you,
   NOT Happy Birthday, dear dumbbell,
   NOT Happy Birthday to you."

I wonder if they have played Pin the Tail on the
Donkey yet? For I am very good at that game.

Uh-oh. Somebody is coming up the stairs. Now
they are walking down the hall. Now they are knock-
ing on my door. I will not answer. Even if they knock
for an hour.

Well, maybe I better open the door. It might be
Sarge.

Ewwww! It's Theodore! With my parents!

It appears they really want me to come down for cake and ice cream.

I must think this over. After all, I have not eaten so much as a morsel of food for over 67 minutes. Therefore, in the interest of saving my life, I will leave my room for some cake and ice cream.

But if it is not chocolate swirl ice cream with hot marshmallow sauce and peanut butter sprinkles on the side and not touching, I will go back to my room. And I will stay there forever.